Fairy
Unicorns

Star Spell

Zanna Davidson

Illustrated by Nuno Alexandre Vieira

Meet the
Unicorns

Zoe

Astra

Sorrel

Unicorn King

Eirra

Orion

Lily

Shadow

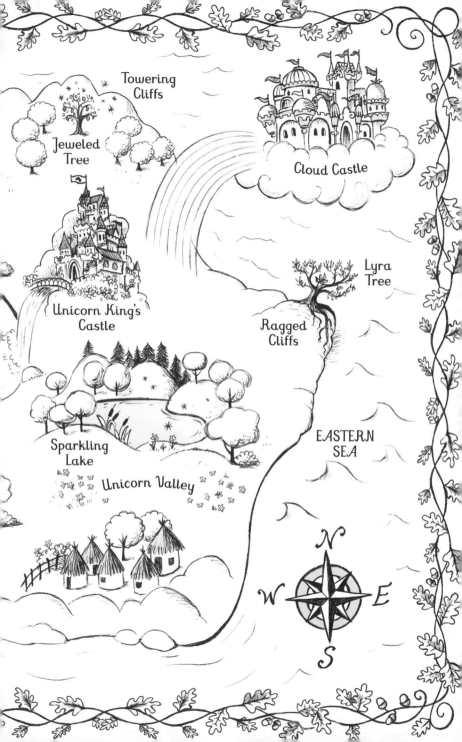

Contents

Chapter One

Zoe sat anxiously on her bed, her heart beating fast as she looked at the moonlight streaming through the bedroom curtains. She was staying at Great-Aunt May's house for the winter vacation and tonight she was going to return to Unicorn Island, the secret world hidden inside the oak tree at the bottom of the garden. Zoe couldn't wait to see her friend

Astra again – the beautiful little unicorn with silvery stars on her coat. But somehow, for the first time ever, Zoe felt nervous about her visit.

Zoe made herself wait until the house was quiet, and she was sure her great-aunt was asleep. Then she crept out of her bedroom, down the stairs and out into the moonlit garden.

When she reached the oak tree, she pulled out her bag of magic dust and

sprinkled a pinch over herself, while chanting the words of a spell:

Let me pass into the magic tree,
Where *fairy* unicorns *fly* wild and *free*.
Show me the trail of sparkling light,
To Unicorn Island, shining bright.

At once came the familiar tingling feeling that started in her toes and in her fingertips. Then she heard the air whooshing around her as she shrank down, down, down to fairy-size. The grass and flowers towered above her, and she could see a light shining through the roots of the oak tree.

Zoe ran down the tunnel, calling out to her friend Astra. As she rounded the corner, she

caught her first glimpse of Unicorn Island —
the beautiful Silvery Glade, its rainbow leaves
swishing in the breeze. And just as before,
Astra was standing there to greet Zoe, her
butterfly wings fluttering and her horn
gleaming pearly white.

"Oh!" Zoe cried, when she reached her,
flinging her arms around the unicorn's silky,
soft neck. "It's really good to see you again,
Astra. I've been thinking about you so much
since my last visit."

"Welcome back," said Astra quietly. Zoe
couldn't help noticing that there was none of
the usual excitement in her voice.

"What is it?" asked Zoe. "Has something
happened?"

"Nothing's happened," Astra replied,

though she kept her eyes down, avoiding Zoe's gaze.

But Zoe knew that something was wrong. "Are you sure?" she asked tentatively. "Is it Shadow? Has he returned?"

Shadow was an evil fairy pony from an island across the sea, who kept plotting to take the Unicorn King's throne and rule Unicorn Island. He'd attacked many times, so far without success. On Zoe's last visit, the king had vowed to defeat Shadow, once and for all.

"No," Astra replied, shaking her head. "There's been no news of Shadow."

The little unicorn didn't say anything more, she just bent down so that Zoe could climb onto her back. Instinctively, Zoe swung her legs over and Astra began trotting through the forest. But Zoe couldn't help feeling strange – as if somehow they had lost their connection.

"Where are we going?" Zoe asked, as they came out of the woods into the lush green valley beyond.

"To a meeting with the king and the Guardians," Astra replied. "Since Shadow destroyed the Unicorn King's Castle, they're using the Rose Bower in the Flower Meadows as a meeting place, and that's where we're headed now. Are you ready to fly?"

"I'm ready," said Zoe. The next moment, Astra began beating her wings and Zoe let out a gasp as they soared away from the valley floor, heading fast into the airy blue. The wind rushed through her hair as Astra swooped through the sky, forcing Zoe to lean down and wrap her arms around Astra's neck.

"You're flying much faster than usual," gasped Zoe. "Are we in a rush?"

"I just want to get to the meeting in time," Astra replied. "I want to hear everything they're going to say about Shadow—"

She broke off abruptly, as if she'd said more

than she intended to. "I'll stop talking now and save my breath for flying."

After that they flew on in silence. Zoe couldn't help gazing towards the Towering Cliffs, where the Unicorn King's Castle had once stood, its turrets rising up above the skyline. She knew all that was left now were bare rocks and the castle's crumbled remains. Zoe's heart sank as she thought of how it had been brought down by Shadow's evil spell. These were troubled times on Unicorn Island. What would Shadow do next?

It was with a jolt that she realized they were nearing the Rose Bower. It was delicately arched and sweet-smelling roses wound around the outside – pink and yellow and creamy

white ones. Astra began to dive towards the
valley floor, wings angled to slow her speed.
She landed in the meadow, directly in
front of the Rose Bower
entrance, her
hoofs gouging
into the soft
earth.

Zoe
slid from
her back and
followed behind Astra as she walked under
the rose-covered arch. Zoe's heart began to
beat fast. She knew this was it…the final
fight to save Unicorn Island started here.

Chapter Two

The arch in the Rose Bower led to a green,
leafy chamber, filled with a gorgeous flowery
scent. In the center stood the Unicorn King
and four of the Guardians: Sorrel, Guardian
of the Trees; Eirra, Guardian of the Snow;
Lily, Guardian of the Flowers, and Nimbus,
Guardian of the Clouds. To the side she could
see Medwen, Guardian of the Spells, and his

apprentice Tio, whose saddlebags were filled with spell books as usual. Zoe smiled with delight. Astra's behavior had unnerved her, but here were more familiar faces and for a moment, everything about Unicorn Island felt right again.

"Welcome," said the king, stepping forward. His expression was grave but Zoe took reassurance from his calm presence. His coat gleamed and his wings and horn were burnished bright, seeming to shine with a light of their own.

Zoe smiled at them all, before giving Astra's mother, Sorrel, a special hug.

"Zoe," Sorrel said. "It's so good to see you

again." But Zoe couldn't help noticing that she kept casting anxious glances at her daughter, and that although Astra smiled at her mother, she didn't walk over to her as she usually would. Sensing Astra wanted to be alone, Zoe went over to stand by Tio.

"Hello," he whispered. "It's good to have you with us, Zoe. These are worrying times." He glanced over his shoulder as he spoke. "See these books?" Tio added. "They're the ones I rescued from the ruins of the castle. I carry them everywhere with me now."

Zoe was desperate to ask Tio about Astra, to see if he'd noticed a change in her too, but the Unicorn King was already calling for silence.

"We've come together to discuss how to

deal with Shadow and his partner, Orion," said the king. "We need to defeat them once and for all. Zoe and Astra, you've battled Orion many times. And, Astra — we haven't forgotten the illuminatrix spell you cast over Shadow. We're hoping you'll both be able to help us."

"I hope so too," said Zoe eagerly.

"Each time Shadow has been defeated," the Unicorn King went on, "we hoped he was gone for good. But we have come to realize that Shadow will stop at nothing."

The Guardians nodded in agreement.

"I have undone the banishment spell keeping them from our shores," the king declared, "and have invited Shadow and Orion to come to Unicorn Island. I know they won't be able to resist the challenge."

There was a collective gasp from the Guardians.

"Why would you do such a thing?" asked Eirra. "Think of the havoc Shadow will cause."

"And the destruction," added Sorrel.

"Are you sure this is a good idea?" asked Lily.

The Unicorn King nodded solemnly. "This way we can fight Shadow face-to-face."

"That's true," agreed Nimbus. "We can use our collective magic – thunderbolts and freezing spells…"

"Exploding clouds and fireblasts," added Medwen.

"That is not my plan," interjected the king.

"There's no spell we can throw at Shadow that he won't be able to fling back at us. After all, he has the Grimoire – our most ancient and powerful spell book. He has been studying it. Shadow is now terrifyingly powerful. And he'll know about the prophecy."

The other Guardians nodded in agreement. Zoe's ears pricked up – a prophecy?

She opened her mouth to ask the Unicorn
King about it, but Sorrel cut in.

"So what do you suggest we do?" she asked.

Zoe turned to look at Astra – her friend
was usually bursting with ideas; it seemed so
strange she was staying silent. But there was
no sign of the little unicorn. Zoe glanced
around the Rose Bower again, wondering if

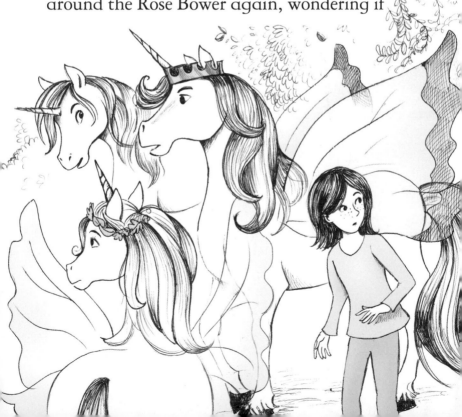

she'd missed her in the shadows.

And that was when she realized something was terribly wrong… Astra had slipped away. Her friend was gone.

The other Guardians were all deep in discussion. None of them seemed to have noticed Astra's disappearance. As quietly as she could, Zoe tiptoed around to the entrance. From the archway, she could see Astra, cantering away across the meadows. For a moment, Zoe hesitated. Should she tell the king and the Guardians what was happening?

With one final look at the Unicorn King, Zoe decided to follow Astra and find out for herself what was going on. Shadow was on his way, but her friend needed her help – she was sure of that.

Outside, Unicorn Island sparkled in the spring sunshine, and it was hard to imagine there was anything wrong. Flowers bobbed their heads amongst the grasses, opening up their petals to the sun. Birds swooped through the sky above her and the air was filled with the sound of their song.

Astra didn't hesitate for a moment, but kept on trotting, as if she knew exactly where she was going. When she reached Moon River, she trotted over the little bridge and headed north. It was then that Zoe saw where Astra was leading her...straight for the ruins of the Unicorn King's Castle.

Zoe followed as the little unicorn's hoofs clattered over the rocks and Zoe's eyes darted left and right, taking in the castle remains.

Smashed turrets and beautiful marbled stones lay strewn around her.

Astra had slowed her pace now and with a sinking feeling, Zoe saw she was headed for a narrow entrance in the cliff face that Zoe had never noticed before.

A moment later, the little unicorn slipped between the rocks and was lost from view.

Taking a deep breath, Zoe too entered the tunnel.

As she stepped inside, the temperature plummeted. It felt cold, damp and heavy. Droplets of water glistened on the black slabs of rock on either side of her and there was only a faint glimmer of light seeping in from outside, just enough to see by. She could hear the tapping of Astra's hoofs ahead of her. Zoe

followed as carefully as she could, not
wanting to make a sound.

Just when she thought the path was
going on forever,
the narrow
passageway
began to open
out to reveal a
cavern, its
walls lit by
burning torches.
Zoe stopped and
ducked behind a
rock, her breath coming in rapid gasps as she
tried to control her panic.

Inside the cavern, greeting Astra like an old
friend, were Orion…and Shadow.

Chapter Three

At first, all Zoe could hear was the rushing in her ears. Why would Astra meet with Shadow and Orion? They were the *enemy*.

"This must be some kind of plan," she told herself. "Astra would never betray the king, the other unicorns…and her own mother."

But at the back of Zoe's mind was another voice, reminding her how strangely Astra had been behaving, ever since she'd arrived back on the island. And Astra had never kept anything secret from her before…

She had to focus. And listen. Zoe craned forward, as far as she dared, peering around the rock so she could catch another glimpse of Astra, Orion and Shadow.

She could see them all standing in the middle of the cavern. Shadow was huge and menacing, with glittering hoofs and, beside him, Orion was only slightly less terrifying. Next to them, Astra looked very small and very vulnerable.

"It's a trap," Astra was saying. "The Unicorn King only lifted the banishment spell so he could defeat you once and for all. The king and the Guardians were working out the best way to fight you when I left. I heard talk of exploding clouds and fireblasts…"

Zoe gasped. *Astra was telling Shadow the king's secrets!*

At Astra's words, Orion snorted in anger. "We thought it was a trap, didn't we, Shadow? We knew there could be no other reason for the king to lift the banishment spell."

Shadow nodded and turned to Astra. "Thank you for your help," he said. His deep voice sent shivers through Zoe's body. She remembered their last encounter, up in the night sky above Unicorn Island. Shadow had trapped her and Astra among the stars, and they'd only escaped after Astra had cast a powerful spell. Could Astra really have

changed her mind now, and joined Shadow's side?

Shadow and Orion had begun speaking in hushed tones, and however hard she tried, Zoe couldn't make out their words. She could still see Astra, her head bowed respectfully.

Then Shadow spoke to Astra once more. "We have tried to take control of Unicorn Island many times but each time our plans have been thwarted. I was worried we'd never succeed." He laughed – a low, humorless sound. "Whatever his intention, the Unicorn King's invitation has come at the perfect time. I've been studying the Grimoire and have mastered the art of overpowering a unicorn's mind. I'll circle the island, casting my spell of enchantment to gather as many unicorns as possible to my side. The king won't stand a chance."

"It's a brilliant plan," said Orion.

Shadow nodded. "I've waited a long time for this moment…" he said. "The chance to crush the king and claim the island as my own."

To Zoe, it was almost as if Shadow was swelling in size as he predicted his victory. His voice echoed around the chamber, filling it with his deep rumble. He pawed the ground as he spoke and tossed his glossy mane. Even hidden in the tunnel, Zoe could feel his power and magic. With Orion and Astra at his side, he seemed unstoppable.

Orion spoke again but his voice was mumbled and to her frustration, Zoe couldn't catch what he said.

"Then it's agreed," said Shadow. "We'll meet by the Ragged Cliffs when we're ready. Astra, stay here for a little while after we've left," he commanded. "We don't want anyone to know you met with us."

Then, to Zoe's horror, she realized Orion and Shadow were getting ready to leave, and the only way out of the cavern was back through the tunnel...where Zoe was standing.

Hearing the clatter of hoofs, Zoe pressed her body back against the cold, slimy surface of the rocks and huddled amongst the shadows, to make herself as small as possible. Shadow and Orion came closer and closer, their snorts growing louder. Their bodies seemed huge as they came into view, and their muscles gleamed beneath their coats. Light glimmered

across Shadow's wings. He looked as if he
could spring into action at any moment.

As he passed her, Zoe began to tremble
with fear. All Shadow had to do was turn to
the side and he'd see her, completely
defenseless against his evil magic. Zoe held
her breath.

Slowly, they walked past, the sound of their hoofs gradually growing fainter and fainter.

Stiffly, Zoe uncurled herself from the wall and checked the passageway, just to be certain that Orion and Shadow really had gone. She had to tell the Guardians what was happening, but as she turned to go, she saw Astra, standing alone in the cavern. Despite everything she'd heard, Zoe couldn't stop herself from hoping that this was all part of Astra's clever plan: that her best friend would never willingly follow Shadow. She had to talk to the little unicorn.

Zoe ran the short distance to the cavern. "Astra!" she cried. "What's happening? What's going on?"

Astra looked up immediately. "How long

have you been there?" she demanded. There was no trace of friendliness in her voice; she sounded cold, accusatory. Zoe's heart sank; Astra's eyes seemed blank in the torchlight, completely without their usual sparkle.

"You must be under some kind of spell," said Zoe, her voice wavering. "Is that it? Has Shadow enchanted you?"

"Of course he hasn't enchanted me," said Astra. "It was my decision. I *chose* to follow Shadow – and if you know what's good for you, you'll follow him too."

Chapter Four

Zoe and Astra gazed at each other across the cavern. Zoe was the first one to speak. "You can't mean it?" she said. "All this time we've been fighting Shadow. Why would you join him now?"

"I've seen that he is right," Astra replied tonelessly. "The Unicorn King is weak and cowardly. Shadow is the one with real power.

Unicorn Island *needs* Shadow."

Astra's words sounded like a chant. With a sickening feeling, Zoe understood how deeply her friend was enchanted.

"You've always been so strong," Zoe said. "How could you let Shadow overpower you? And what about betraying your mother, and our friendship? Doesn't that mean anything?" she added, tears sliding down her cheeks.

"Shadow has promised to make me the most powerful unicorn on the island. He's going to teach me all the magic he knows. That's the most important thing now."

"But it's the wrong *kind* of magic, Astra, can't you see that? He's learned all the most evil spells from the Grimoire."

"Is it wrong?" said Astra, softly. "Perhaps

you don't know me as well as you thought you did."

"That's not true," said Zoe. In desperation, she reached out to touch Astra, to stroke or hug her, anything to bring back the Astra she knew…but Astra jerked away.

"If you're not going to join Shadow, then what are you going to do now?" asked Astra. There was something in her eyes that made

Zoe take a step backwards, towards the cavern wall.

"I…I don't know," said Zoe.

"You're going to go back and tell the king about this, aren't you?" Astra went on. "And then you're all going to try and stop Shadow. Well, I won't let you!"

Zoe's back was almost against the rocky wall now. She knew she should feel scared of Astra when she was like this – but Zoe couldn't bring herself to believe that her friend would really hurt her.

"I'm going to make sure nothing gets in Shadow's way," said Astra, her voice almost like a hiss.

Then the little unicorn turned and galloped out of the cavern.

"Wait!" Zoe called, dashing after her. But as she reached the start of the tunnel there was a deep rumbling sound and it seemed as if the whole cavern was starting to shake. Zoe stumbled backwards just as huge boulders began to fall from the cavern walls, crashing down before her, filling the narrow entrance.

"No!" cried Zoe. "Astra…if that's you casting a spell, please…stop!"

The rockfall seemed to last

forever, and the sound of stone grinding against stone echoed around the walls. Then at last, with a final flurry of small stones, the rocks stopped falling and there was nothing but silence.

Zoe dashed forward and began trying to lift the rocks with her bare hands. But they were at least twice her size and there was nothing she could do to move them. The boulders had blocked her only way out. There was no escape.

I'm trapped here, she realized. *And no one is going to tell the Unicorn King what's happening.*

Then, from the other side of the wall, she heard the murmur of a voice.

A terrifying thought struck her... What if it was Shadow? What if he had come back for her?

Shaking with fear, Zoe crouched behind one of the boulders and waited. One by one, the rocks began to move. Slowly, a figure began to appear at the mouth of the cave...

At first, it appeared only in silhouette, blacked out by the light from behind. But Zoe dared to hope... This figure wasn't big enough to be Shadow. Could it be Astra, come back to save her after all?

She crept forward, then nearly laughed out loud in relief as she recognized the scruffy mane sticking out in all directions, and the saddlebags bulging with books.

"Tio! Tio!" cried Zoe, and she ran the rest of the way towards him, flinging her arms around his soft neck. "Oh! You have no idea how glad I am to see you."

"Well," said Tio, his voice full of pride. "I'm very glad to see you too."

"But how did you find me?" asked Zoe. "I followed Astra – and found her here with Orion and Shadow! Can you believe it? Tio, it's terrible, but it's true…Astra's on Shadow's side." The words tumbled out of her mouth.

"We know about Astra," Tio replied, stopping Zoe in her tracks. "The Unicorn King has suspected something ever since Astra fought Shadow in the night sky."

"Ever since *then?*" gasped Zoe. "But I don't remember Shadow casting a spell of enchantment over Astra... Though I do remember that afterwards Astra said she felt strange. And she was very quiet..."

"The king believes Astra fought Shadow in anger. Shadow will have used that anger to draw her in and begin a spell of enchantment over Astra, so that she would turn to his side. The king told Sorrel his suspicions, but she refused to believe him. She couldn't bear the thought of Astra joining Shadow."

Zoe gasped. "But if the Unicorn King knew all this, why did he invite Astra to the meeting in the Rose Bower? He must have known she was going to betray him."

Tio nodded. "Exactly. That was all part of

the king's plan. He wanted Astra to lead us to Shadow. He cast a spell on her, so that wherever she went, she'd leave an invisible trail. All I had to do was cast a little spell of my own to reveal the trail, and then I followed her right here."

Zoe shook her head to clear her thoughts. Everything was happening so fast. "Okay," she said, taking a deep breath. "So what happens now?"

"Follow me," said Tio, and he began leading Zoe back out of the cave. "I have instructions to take you straight to the king. Eirra and Lily are already secretly following Shadow, and Nimbus and Sorrel are letting the other unicorns know what's happening."

They were nearing the end of the tunnel

now and Zoe was momentarily dazzled by the bright daylight, after the dark cavern.

"We must hurry," Tio said gently. "Here," he added, bending his forelegs as he spoke. "Climb on my back."

Zoe swung herself onto his back, gripping his mane with her fingers. It seemed strange to be riding a unicorn who wasn't Astra. She missed everything about her friend – the silky softness of her coat, the way her eyes lit up whenever she had one of her ideas…

Tio began cantering, out from beneath the cliffs, his saddlebags bumping along his back. But before he could take flight, they saw the Unicorn King swooping in towards them, his horn glinting in the sunlight, wings outstretched. Behind him came Medwen,

Guardian of the Spells, his expression grave.

"Well done, Tio," said the king, as he landed beside them. "Thank you for helping Zoe."

Then he turned to Zoe. "Do you have any news for us? We saw Shadow and Orion, and then Astra, emerge from the cave."

"Yes, Your Majesty," said Zoe. "I was in the cave with them – hiding. Astra told Shadow that you'd invited Shadow and Orion here as a trick," she continued, knowing how important it was to remember everything. "They didn't seem surprised. In fact, Shadow said this had come at the perfect time. He said he's studied the Grimoire and learned to overpower a unicorn's mind, and that he's going to gather an army of unicorns to fight

against you. They've agreed to meet on the Ragged Cliffs when they're ready to do battle."

Zoe couldn't read the Unicorn King's expression as he took in this news. He simply nodded his head. Zoe felt soothed, sensing the king's strength and power.

The Unicorn King turned to face Medwen. "Take this news to the other Guardians. When they have gathered as many unicorns as they can, we will also meet on the Ragged Cliffs. If we get there first, we can fight from the clifftops and force Shadow and his army to fight from the air, which will tire them. We must act quickly."

"Yes, Your Majesty," said Medwen. With those words he took flight again, soaring into the sky on beating wings, his tail streaming out behind him.

"Now," said the Unicorn King, turning to Zoe and Tio. "The time has come to meet Shadow on the Ragged Cliffs. Let's fly there together."

Chapter Five

As one, they took to the skies, the Unicorn
King leading the way to the Ragged Cliffs.
He powered over the island on smooth, steady
wing beats, the sun's rays glancing off his
coat, his head held high and proud. Tio flew
as fast as he could to keep up and Zoe clung
tightly to him, taking comfort in his warmth.
But even as she worried about the fight that

lay ahead with Shadow, she couldn't stop thinking about Astra.

"What will happen to Astra?" she asked the king, her voice carrying on the wind.

He turned to her. "Have faith in your friend," he said. "I will not give up hope that she will return to us. And believe me, I will do everything in my power to make sure she doesn't come to any harm."

As they flew, Zoe couldn't help remembering her first trip to the Ragged Cliffs, with Astra. The island looked just the same, but for the empty space where the Unicorn King's Castle had once stood. Below them, the Sparkling Lake shone in the sunshine, its still waters reflecting back a perfect image of their flight.

And then she felt a stirring in the air, as if
something momentous was happening.
Looking down, she saw unicorn after unicorn
taking to the air and joining them as they
journeyed to the Ragged Cliffs. She could see
Cloud Unicorns streaming down from Cloud

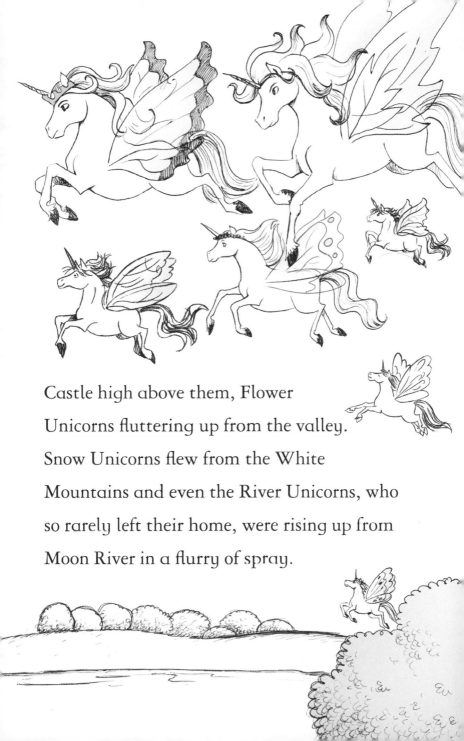

Castle high above them, Flower
Unicorns fluttering up from the valley.
Snow Unicorns flew from the White
Mountains and even the River Unicorns, who
so rarely left their home, were rising up from
Moon River in a flurry of spray.

They all came together on the clifftops, thronging around the Unicorn King as he landed. They all looked as if they were readying themselves for battle, pawing the ground and tossing their manes, their horns sparking with magic. Tio carefully took off his saddlebags and placed them on the ground. He was getting ready for action.

Zoe spotted that Sorrel had returned from following Shadow and was standing among the other unicorns. She seemed to be looking around, her eyes darting this way and that, and Zoe knew she was searching for Astra, hoping that she had come to join them after all.

"As you have all heard, Shadow is on the island," the Unicorn King began, his voice strong but calm. "He'll soon arrive here with an army of followers – all the unicorns that he's been able to enchant. Those unicorns are our friends and family, but it is right that we defend ourselves. Shadow *must* be stopped. And what I ask of you now is not to *fight* Shadow, but for each of you to use your special powers to block his spells."

"Flower Unicorns – return his attacks with storms of petals. Cloud Unicorns – blow them away with wind charms. River Unicorns – defeat his magic with jets of water, and Snow Unicorns, freeze his spells before they can reach us. If we keep doing this, and don't give up, Shadow will see that he cannot win, and that good will always defeat evil."

There were murmurings among the unicorns as they discussed the king's words.

Eventually, a large Snow Unicorn came to the front of the crowd. "But why can't we use our powerful spells to *attack* Shadow?" he asked. "Our numbers will likely be greater. Surely our collective power could defeat him?"

"Yes!" called another unicorn. "Let's fight him properly."

"Then we can end this quickly!" called a third.

"That is not the way," said the king, his voice rumbling across the cliffs. Zoe had never heard him sound so stern. "If you fight in anger, Shadow will be able to use that anger against you. He'll cast a spell of enchantment over you, as he has done with young Astra… As he's doing now with many other unicorns. Fighting him that way will not achieve anything."

There was a chorus of assent. "We'll do as you say," said the large Snow Unicorn.

"Then prepare yourselves," replied the Unicorn King, his eyes fixed on the horizon. "Shadow and Orion are on their way."

Zoe followed his gaze and spotted Shadow's unmistakable outline – his long mane, the broad back and huge, spiky wings. He came powering across the sky towards them, silhouetted against the low sun. Beside him flew Orion on glittering wings, and on his other side was Astra, snowy white, the stars on her coat sparkling. And they weren't alone. Shadow had cast his enchantment over many other unicorns, and they thronged behind him, their eyes all as blank and staring as Astra's.

There were gasps from the unicorns on the Ragged Cliffs, at the sight of their friends, following in Shadow's wake.

"Only now do I believe it," said Sorrel, closely watching Astra as she flew at Shadow's side.

"I wouldn't have believed it either," said Zoe, from astride Tio's back. "Until I saw it for myself. But, Sorrel, she's under a spell. Her eyes are blank…it looks like Astra but it's not *her*."

"We'll get Astra back," Sorrel said fiercely. "I won't let Shadow take my daughter from me."

With those words she rose up into the air, looking as if she was going to aim straight for Shadow.

"Come back, Sorrel," said the Unicorn King,

his command drawing her back down to the clifftop. "You must have faith. We'll win Astra back, I promise. But now is not the time to try and save her."

Zoe could see how torn Sorrel was – longing to go after her daughter, but knowing that the Unicorn King spoke the truth. She felt the same longing to drop everything and rescue her friend.

"Ready, everyone?" cried the king.

"Ready!" came the reply.

But a sharp crack rent the air and the next moment, Unicorn Island was plunged into darkness.

There was a collective gasp, then unicorns were crying out in uproar and confusion. It was black except for the spells which crackled and sparkled through the air, like colored lightning.

"What's happening?" cried Zoe, clinging tightly to Tio's mane. "What's going on?"

"This must be Shadow's work," said Tio. "He must want the darkness as a cover for his plans."

"Stay calm and stand together," commanded the Unicorn King, his voice ringing through the noise around him. "Shadow is only trying to scare us."

Then he began to chant a spell of his own.

Cover of darkness, hear my cry,
Fold back your edges and let fly.
On beating wings, a butterfly,
To take the blackness from our sky.

Gazing up, Zoe let out a gasp of surprise. Before their eyes, the sky was transformed into a giant butterfly, its wings midnight black. Even as it took form, it swooped away, flying across the island, leaving the clear light of day behind it.

"I've never seen the king do a spell like that," said Zoe.

"He's not one to show off his magic," said Tio, admiringly, "but when he does, he leaves you in no doubt of his powers."

Hovering in the air, not far from the cliff edge, Shadow snorted in rage. His followers were fanned out behind him, beating their wings in time. "Tricks!" Shadow cried, angrily. "Nothing but tricks. I'll show you!"

And the next moment, a series of

thunderbolts began heading straight for the Ragged Cliffs.

The Unicorn King muttered another spell, catching the thunderbolts in a thick purple cloud, but one burst through and hit the cliff under them. Zoe could feel the ground shuddering beneath her feet and heard part of the cliff edge crumble away.

In a flurry of wing beats, Nimbus, Eirra, Sorrel, Lily and Naida surged forwards until they surrounded the king.

"We see what Shadow is doing," said Nimbus, his voice grim. "He's aiming straight for you, Your Majesty."

"We will stay by your side to protect you," added Lily.

Zoe could only watch in wonder as the

Guardians and the king battled the spells of Shadow and his followers. Eirra breathed out snowflakes by the hundred, freezing the fireballs and stopping them in their tracks.

Nimbus blew back the

thunderbolts and daggers of ice,

while Lily smothered the spells with swirling

clouds of petals. Sorrel raised her horn and

turned the enchantments to harmless,

fluttering leaves. The other unicorns joined in as best they could, casting spells of their own to block the onslaught of dark magic.

"I think we're winning," said Zoe, excitedly. "The king's plan might just work. Shadow and his army must tire soon. They can't keep hovering and casting spells forever."

But every now and then a fireball or thunderbolt would break through the Guardians' defenses and whiz through the air above them.

"I really don't like battles," said Tio, watching a stray thunderbolt hurtle towards the ground. "I wish I was back in the castle Spell Room. Being inside is so much safer. Oh goodness!" he added, a moment later, looking directly ahead.

Zoe looked up, and saw a fireball heading straight for them. "Watch out, Tio!" she cried.

Tio was forced up into the air on fluttering wings, but as he tried to land again on the Ragged Cliffs, another fireball followed in its wake. Tio twisted this way and that and Zoe had to do everything she could just to stay on him.

"Oh no!" Zoe said suddenly. "Tio – the fireballs! They're from Shadow. He's not coming for the king any more. He's after us!"

"Why would he come after us?" cried Tio.
"We're not Guardians. That can't be right…"

But it was. Shadow was powering towards
them, sending fireballs thick and fast. Tio
frantically muttered spells beneath his
breath, trying to stop the onslaught with
freezing clouds of ice, but Zoe could tell they
were in trouble.

Tio's movements became more and more
frantic as fireballs whizzed past them, some
within touching distance.

"We need help!" said Zoe, unable to hide
her fear. "I'm going to fall off, Tio, with you
moving like this."

Shadow was only a short distance away
from them now, and Zoe could hear the deep,
menacing rumble of his laughter as he fired

off another fireball. This one was bigger than all the others and Tio was forced to rear steeply upwards to avoid it.

"Hooray!" cried Tio, as he rose almost vertically into the sky. "It missed!"

"Oh…Tio!" Zoe cried out. His movement had been so fast, and so jerky, she had lost her grip on him. And then she felt herself, as if in slow motion, sliding off his back and falling, falling…

Chapter Six

Zoe plummeted through the air, calling for help as she fell.

Tio started after her, but Shadow cast a spell trapping him in a shimmering, magical net. Then he pulled Tio across the sky, far away from Zoe.

Zoe could see the Ragged Cliffs rushing towards her and then she was tumbling past

them, whooshing down the side
of the cliff face. She reached
out with her hands,
desperately trying to grab
hold of something…anything…
and let out a cry of relief as she
caught hold of some
tree roots, trailing the cliff face.

But the roots were only slender
and Zoe realized they weren't
going to hold her for long. Even
as she gripped on for dear life, her
hands sweaty against the wood,
the smaller roots were breaking
under her weight. Zoe looked
down and gulped. The ground was
very far away, and there was

nothing at the bottom to break her fall.

Then a shadow passed over her. Looking up, Zoe could see Astra, circling in the air above her.

"Astra, please!" she called. "Please help me."

The biggest root began to crack and Zoe thought she saw something flash in Astra's eyes. The next moment, the little unicorn was zooming towards her at full speed. "Onto my back, Zoe!" she cried, hovering beneath her.

With relief, Zoe let go of the root and slipped onto Astra's back. Then, without another word, she wrapped her arms around Astra's silky, soft neck.

"You saved me!" cried Zoe, her body trembling with shock and relief.

Fireballs and thunderbolts were still

whizzing through the air around them and Astra looked around, wondering where to go. "We can't stay here, it's not safe," she said. "And I don't want Shadow to see me with you or he'll be after both of us…"

"Over there!" cried Zoe, pointing to a small ledge further down the cliff face, slightly hidden beneath overhanging rock.

Astra dived down to land on it and Zoe slid from Astra's back, gazing deep into her eyes.

"The enchantment has broken, hasn't it?" she said, hardly daring to hope.

Astra nodded. "It has…" she said, her voice wobbling. "When I saw you fall, it was as if I came back to myself. I knew I had to break through Shadow's spell and do whatever I could to save you."

"I'm so glad," said Zoe, hugging her. "I thought I'd lost you forever."

"I'm so sorry," Astra replied. "I…"

But Zoe interrupted before she could say more. "None of that is important now," she said. "We have to stop Shadow. The Unicorn King thinks we can defeat him just by stopping his spells, but I'm not so sure. I can't imagine Shadow giving up. All I know is that we can't fight him in anger."

"That's true," Astra replied. "There must be another way."

For a moment they both watched the battle above them. Spells were whizzing back and forth, the air thick with magic and smoke and flying unicorns. But the ledge they were standing on was a narrow one, and they had to press their bodies against the cliff face to stop themselves from falling.

"Well we can't stay here," Zoe said, gazing down as a small part of the ledge crumbled under their weight. "I don't want to fall again. And if we're forced to take flight suddenly, we might be seen."

"Just a moment," said Astra, her brow furrowed in thought.

"What is it?" asked Zoe. "Have you had an idea?"

Astra nodded. "How about if instead of just

blocking Shadow's spells, we make them rebound back on to him? That way we're not using our own anger, just sending his anger back at him."

"Brilliant!" said Zoe. "Do you know a rebounding spell?"

"I do...but it's not powerful enough."

The little unicorn looked across at where the Unicorn King's Castle had once stood. "I could have made it work with the magic mirror," she said. "There was one in the Spell Room, but it was destroyed when Shadow sent the star-quake."

"We can't be this close and fail now," said Zoe, thinking hard. And as her gaze followed Astra's, looking down at the ruined castle, she caught a glimpse of the Sparkling Lake, reflecting back the light from the fireballs and thunderbolts in the sky above them.

"The lake!" she cried. "It's glassy…and still, like a giant mirror. Would that work?"

"Of course, the Sparkling Lake!" said Astra, her voice full of hope.

"So we just need to get Shadow to cast his most powerful spell towards the lake," prompted Zoe. "And then you can get it to bounce back at him! Only I'm not sure how we do that…"

"I do! Quick! Onto my back," said Astra, already fluttering her wings. "I'll explain as we fly."

Zoe swung herself onto Astra's back and they flew towards the top of the Ragged Cliffs, dodging and ducking fiery spells as they went.

"Keep an eye out for Shadow," cried Astra. "It's very important he doesn't see us together."

As they flew over the unicorns on the clifftops, Zoe could see their anxious expressions. More and more of the evil magic seemed to be getting through. "Oh no," she cried. "It really does look like Shadow's winning."

"Then there's not a moment to lose," said Astra, as she came in to land. "Quick! Go and find the Unicorn King. Tell him to meet me above the middle of the Sparkling Lake, and to keep very still when he gets there. When I send a light from my horn, that's his signal to fly back towards the cliffs – and fast."

"And where are you going?" asked Zoe, as she slid from Astra's back.

"To talk to Shadow," Astra replied. "To tell him that I've tricked the king into meeting him in the middle of the Sparkling Lake. I just hope he believes me..."

Zoe watched Astra swoop away, then began to run towards the Unicorn King, ducking the firebolts whizzing towards her. The King was just where she'd left him, standing proud and tall, battling tirelessly against the spells of Shadow and his followers. He was surrounded by a flank of Guardians but they parted when they saw Zoe. "Your Majesty," cried Zoe, as she reached his side.

The Unicorn King glanced down at her, spells still sparkling from his horn.

"What is it?" he asked. His breath sounded ragged, as if defending Shadow's spells was using every ounce of his energy.

"Astra and I have worked out a way to defeat Shadow," Zoe began.

There was a flash in the king's eyes. "Go on," he said. "You have my full attention, but

I must keep my eyes on the battle."

Zoe took a deep breath. "Astra is on our side again," she went on. "She broke through Shadow's enchantment."

"Are you sure?" asked the king.

"I'm sure," Zoe replied. "Please – you have to trust us. Will you fly to the middle of the Sparkling Lake and wait there? Then, as soon as you see a flash of light from Astra's horn… that's your signal to head back to the cliffs. Astra plans to catch Shadow with his own spell."

All this time, the Guardians had never stopped firing their spells, but it was clear they had overheard the plan.

"You can't go, Your Majesty," said Eirra. "This could easily be one of Shadow's tricks.

How do we know Astra is to be trusted?"

"I swear she is," said Zoe, imploringly. "I could see it in her eyes. That blank look had gone. She was back to her old self!"

"Oh I hope you're right," said Sorrel, her voice wavering slightly. "But if you're wrong, the king's life could be at stake."

"I agree with Eirra," said Nimbus. "Don't go, Your Majesty. Let's stick with our original plan and just keep blocking the spells. Shadow has to tire soon."

"I will go," said the Unicorn King, gravely. "I believe in Zoe and Astra, and Shadow is not tiring. He is even stronger than we realized. This is the only way. Zoe, climb on my back. We'll leave at once."

Zoe did as he asked, even as Lily protested.

"You could be walking into a trap!"

The Unicorn King turned to them. "This could also be the moment predicted by the Grimoire – the prophecy," he said.

Zoe wondered at the king's words again. What was the prophecy? But there was no time to ask. "Can you be sure about the prophecy?" called Sorrel, as the king took flight.

"No," the king called back. "But it's a risk I'm willing to take. We must do everything we can to save the island, and I believe that this is our last chance."

Chapter Seven

The Unicorn King and Zoe left the Ragged Cliffs and began to fly towards the Sparkling Lake. All around them, spells whizzed through the air, but the king didn't stop for a moment.

The closer they came to the lake, the tighter Zoe gripped onto his mane. Shadow was waiting for them, hovering over the middle of the lake, looking more terrifying than ever, his expression gloating. Astra was by his side and Zoe tried desperately not to catch her eye.

"So you really came?" Shadow said, with a hollow laugh. And then he began to chant beneath his breath.

I summon up my deepest powers,
Channeled from my darkest hours.
I strike the king, I make him fall,
Now he's powerless, weak and small…

As he raised his head to strike the spell, Zoe could hear Astra frantically muttering a spell of her own.

Sparkling Lake, rebound this spell,

Send it back, make it swell.

Strike Shadow, so he's small,

Save the king, let Shadow fall...

And just as a bolt of light shot from
Shadow towards the Unicorn King, Astra sent
out a small light of her own.

"Now, Your Majesty!" Zoe cried. "Move!"

The king veered away, narrowly missing
the bolt of light, which shot down, down,
towards the Sparkling Lake. It hit the surface
of the water with a flash of color and
rebounded back towards Shadow, moving
even faster than before. With a strange, high-
pitched sizzling sound it collided with Shadow
and then, before Zoe's amazed eyes, Shadow

let out a cry of shock and surprise…and
began to shrink.

At once, the Unicorn King began chanting:

Find him, bind him,

safe in a cage.

Snatch him, trap him,

contain his rage…

When Zoe looked
again, the tiny
figure of Shadow
was trapped inside
a cage of magical
vines. The king

dived towards it as it plummeted towards the
lake and caught one of the vines between his

teeth. Then he flew with it, back to the Ragged Cliffs, Astra following close behind.

Shadow's followers cried out in shock and confusion, the blank look slowly draining from their eyes. As it dawned on them what had happened, they hovered anxiously above the cliffs.

"We've done it," said the Unicorn King, after he had placed the cage on the ground. "We've really done it. Shadow can no longer harm us."

Sliding from his back, Zoe caught his eye and smiled.

The Guardians, and the other unicorns on the cliffs, stepped forward. There was a moment of awed silence, as if no one could believe it had really happened. They all gazed at Shadow, thrashing against the bars of his cage.

"Is he still magic?" asked Astra. "Does he still have his powers?"

"No," replied the king. "The spell Shadow cast was made to rob me of all my magic. And now that's his fate."

"You've really beaten him," said Nimbus, breaking into a wide smile. "Congratulations, Your Majesty."

"Don't thank me," said the Unicorn King. "We owe our gratitude to Astra and Zoe."

"Three cheers for Astra and Zoe!" cried a voice from the crowd, and all along the Ragged Cliffs, the unicorns cheered and stamped their hoofs, until the cliffs echoed with the sound.

Looking around, Zoe saw that the unicorns who had joined with Shadow were now landing on the cliffs around them, bowing down to the Unicorn King. All, that is, except for Orion, who hung back, hovering in the air with a guarded, watchful expression.

"We're sorry, Your Majesty," said a River Unicorn, as he touched down before the king. "We're sorry we let you down." As one, they moved to stand before the Unicorn King and bent their heads in shame.

"No one is to be blamed," he replied, his gaze taking in all the unicorns. "Shadow's magic was incredibly powerful, his spell of enchantment almost impossible to resist. Now is a time only for celebration – that together we have defeated Shadow, once and for all."

Zoe caught Astra's eye. "Your plan worked," she said, grinning at her.

"With your help," Astra replied.

"We always did make a great team," said Zoe, and she reached over to give Astra another hug.

She only let go when she heard Tio calling out her name. He rushed over to her, his mane sticking out more than ever. "Oh!" he cried. "Thank goodness you're all right, Zoe. I was so worried when you fell from my back, and then I wanted to go after you, but Shadow..."

"I know, I know," Zoe reassured him, reaching out to stroke his neck.

"Well," Tio went on, "I'm just not a unicorn who is made for action. The sooner I can get back to my spell books, the better."

Then silence fell and looking around, Zoe realized that Orion had flown down to join them on the clifftops. The other unicorns glared at him, full of hostility. Orion bowed low before the Unicorn King.

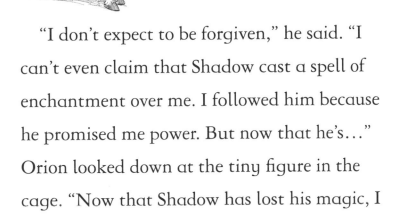

"I don't expect to be forgiven," he said. "I can't even claim that Shadow cast a spell of enchantment over me. I followed him because he promised me power. But now that he's..." Orion looked down at the tiny figure in the cage. "Now that Shadow has lost his magic, I feel relieved. I want nothing more than to serve you again, Your Majesty."

For a moment the Unicorn King just stared at him. "I forgive you," he said at last. "I want nothing more than to see you serve the island as a Guardian again. I have always valued your clever mind and your magic. It was a hard blow when you joined with Shadow. It will take time for you to prove your loyalty to us again."

"I understand," said Orion. He gazed around at the Guardians. None of them came forward, but one by one they nodded their heads, as if in agreement with the king.

"I'll leave you to your celebrations," the large unicorn continued. "I am going to head to the mountains. Now is the time for me to be on my own. But I hope, one day, to be able to join you again."

With those words, Orion beat his wings and took to the skies, a lone figure against the setting sun.

"We're safe at last," said Sorrel, nuzzling Astra, who was back at her side. "I can hardly believe it. But best of all is having you back, Astra. I missed you."

"I missed you too, Mom," said Astra. "I'm sorry about everything that happened."

"Well, today you've proved yourself as loyal and true," said the Unicorn King, smiling at her. "And you proved your magic, too. From now on it will always be there when you need it. And now there is only one thing left to do." He fluttered up into the air and

aimed his horn at
the rocks below,
where his castle
had once stood.
There was a flash
of light, a rushing

sound as if a waterfall were being pulled back
towards its source, and then a cry from the
watching unicorns.

"The castle!" said Zoe. "It's back! It's really
back!"

And there it was – its marbled surface
white and gleaming against the rock face, the
flag fluttering in the breeze. Once more, ivy
trailed from its turrets and roses arched over
the great door.

"I could only bring back the castle once the

threat of Shadow was truly over,"
said the Unicorn King. "We have nothing
to fear from him now."

Zoe looked from the castle to Shadow's
cage. Then, unable to resist, she bent down, so
she could gaze in at Shadow between the bars.
"He's so small," she said, "and so powerless.

It's almost impossible to believe he did all this."

"I so nearly defeated you," the tiny Shadow hissed. Zoe held his gaze, refusing to look away.

"What are you going to do with him now, Your Majesty?" asked Astra.

"I'm not sure," the Unicorn King replied, thoughtfully. "He may look harmless, but he can never be trusted."

As he spoke, he looked over at Zoe, a questioning expression in his eyes. He didn't say anything but somehow Zoe guessed at once what he was thinking.

"Do you want me to take Shadow back to

my world?" she asked. "Then you'd never have to worry about him again."

"Would you do that for us?" the king replied. "Then Unicorn Island would truly be safe. But I would think no less of you if you don't want to take him."

"I'll take him," said Zoe, without a moment's doubt. "I'll make sure he never returns to Unicorn Island." She knew it was an important task, but at last she felt she had her own role to play, without magic, to keep Unicorn Island safe.

"But what about the Grimoire?" asked Astra. "We still need to get it back…"

"I have heard that Shadow has hidden it on an island beyond our own," replied the Unicorn King.

"Then I'm going to make it my mission to track it down," said Astra.

"And I'll help you," added Zoe.

"Well, we'll see about that," said Sorrel. "Don't you think you two have had enough adventures?" But Zoe could see how proudly she looked at Astra.

"Now, Zoe," said Sorrel, turning towards her. "It is time for you to return to your own world. Night is drawing in and we all need a rest after the battle."

"Sorrel is right," added the king. "It is time for you to leave."

"I wish I didn't have to go..." said Zoe. "But before I do, I have one last question. In the Rose Bower, and on the cliffs, you said something about a prophecy. What did you mean by that? How did you know to trust Astra and me?"

The king smiled in reply. "It is written in the Grimoire that Unicorn Island would one day come under attack by an enemy from across the seas. But it is also written that the island would be saved by a human child and a unicorn with stars on her coat. That's why Shadow wanted to capture Astra so badly and make sure you were out of the way. I always hoped the prophecy would come true…and it did."

Zoe and Astra gasped, both feeling overwhelmed by a strange mixture of awe and confusion. "We were part of a *prophecy*?" asked Zoe. They looked at each other in wonderment, and Zoe felt the strength of their connection return.

"I never could have dreamed it," said Astra. "I always thought I was just a unicorn who couldn't do magic."

Then she bent her legs and Zoe swung herself onto her back one last time, still clutching Shadow's cage.

"Goodbye, Zoe," said Sorrel. "And once again, thank you for all your help. We never could have defeated Shadow without you."

"We would each like to give you a present," said Lily, coming forwards. "In return for all that you have done for us." She presented Zoe with a rose-petal cloak that floated towards her and settled across her shoulders.

"Oh! It's beautiful. Thank you!" cried Zoe.

Then one by one, each of the Guardians stepped forward to give Zoe a gift. From Eirra, she received a circlet made of glittering crystals of ice that would never melt. From Sorrel, a necklace of rainbow leaves. From Naida, a pouch of glittering river dust, so that she would always be able to breathe in the waters of Moon River. And from Nimbus, a beautiful, sparkling statue of Cloud Castle.

Zoe was wreathed in smiles.

"You are always welcome on Unicorn Island, Zoe," said the king. "I have one final gift for you." He handed her a tiny, golden bell. "Ring this if you need us, and wherever we are, we will come to you."

"Thank you, all of you," said Zoe. Then Astra beat her wings and they soared into the sky. As Zoe turned to give a final wave to the unicorns on the clifftop she saw a series of sparkles shoot from the Guardians' horns. The next moment a message lit the darkening sky.

In huge letters, it read:

Thank you, Zoe!

"Oh!" cried Zoe, as a cheer went up from all the other unicorns. "I never expected this."

"You deserve it," said Astra, with a smile. "You have been a true friend to all of us."

As they sped back over the island, Zoe was

glad that it was just her and Astra, alone together. She wrapped her arms around the little unicorn, breathing in her warm honey scent.

All too soon, the passageway to the Great Oak came into view and Astra fluttered down to the ground.

"Goodbye, Zoe," she said. "Promise me you'll come again soon?"

"I promise," Zoe replied.

With one last hug, Zoe began to run back down the tunnel, until she emerged into Great-Aunt May's garden. For a moment, the grasses and flowers towered above her and then she was growing bigger and bigger, until she was back to her normal size. But the gifts from the unicorns, she realized, had remained

fairy-sized. In her hand, she held a tiny silver circlet, a cloak of flowers, a golden bell and a necklace of rainbow leaves. And there was Shadow, a tiny fairy pony, in the palm of her hand. He would be a reminder for always that her adventures had been more than just dreams.

Edited by Becky Walker

Designed by Brenda Cole

Reading consultant: Alison Kelly

Digital Manipulation by Nick Wakeford

First published in 2017 by Usborne Publishing Ltd.,
Usborne House, 83-85 Saffron Hill, London EC1N 8RT, England.
www.usborne.com

Copyright © Usborne Publishing, 2017

Illustrations copyright © Usborne Publishing, 2017

This edition first published in America in 2018

Front cover and inside illustrations by Nuno Vieira Alexandre

The name Usborne and the devices ♀ 🎈 are Trade Marks of
Usborne Publishing Ltd.

A CIP catalogue record for this book is available from the British Library.